MEET THE GIRL TALK CHARACTERS

Sabrina Wells is petite, with curly auburn hair, sparkling hazel eyes, and a bubbly personality. Sabrina loves magazines, shopping, sleepovers, and most of all, she loves talking to her best friends.

Katie Campbell is a straight-A student and super athlete. With her blond hair, blue eyes, and matching clothes, she's everyone's idea of Little Miss Perfect. But Katie has a few surprises for everyone, including herself!

Randy Zak has just moved to Acorn Falls from New York City, and is she ever cool! With her radical spiked haircut and her hip New York clothes, Randy teaches everyone just how much fun it is to be different.

Allison Cloud is a Native American Indian. Allison's supersmart and really beautiful. But she has one major problem: She's thirteen years old, five foot seven, and still growing!

BABY TALK

By L. E. Blair

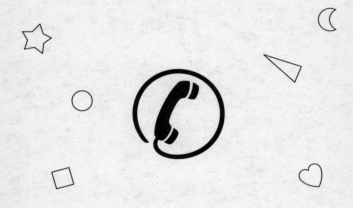

GIRL TALK® series created by Western Publishing Company, Inc.

Western Publishing Company, Inc., Racine, Wisconsin 53404

R MCMXCIV

Text by B. B. Calhoun

Chapter One

"I'm a race car driver — watch out! Vroooom! Vrooooooooom!"

I sighed as my little brother, Charlie, ran out of our kitchen and into the den. He was wearing a green football helmet on his head, and around his waist he held a large cardboard carton with a hole cut in the bottom for his legs to come through.

"Charlie!" I called, tossing my long, black braid over my shoulder. "Charlie, put your race car away and come finish your cereal!"

It was Monday morning, and I was trying to get my seven-year-old brother ready for school. My mother was still upstairs in bed. She was going to have a baby soon, and my father had said she needed all the rest she could get.

Meanwhile I could hear Charlie running around in the den. "Vrooooom-vroooom! Vrooomvroom!"

I had helped him make his cardboard "race car" last weekend while I was baby-sitting for him. We had painted it red together and put a big black "7" on each side. At the time, it had seemed like a great way to keep him busy while my parents went out to dinner. But now I was beginning to wish I had never come up with the project.

I shook my head. How was I going to get Charlie to finish his breakfast? Oh, well, at least I was going to finish eating. I spooned the rest of my cereal into my mouth, picked up my bowl, and took it over to the sink.

I was tempted to call my grandmother up on the phone and ask her to help me with Charlie. But I knew she wasn't up yet. Ever since she and my grandfather retired, they've liked to sleep late. My grandmother says it's the one nice thing she can do for herself. My grandparents live in an apartment attached to the back of our house, and I must admit it is nice having my grandparents so close. But I knew I couldn't disturb them just to come and get Charlie to eat his breakfast.

Suddenly my father stuck his head in the kitchen door.

"I'm off," he announced. "I have to be at the

reservation to meet with a client by nine."

I knew my father was talking about the Chippewa Reservation forty miles away. Our family is Native American Chippewa, and my father grew up on the reservation. Now he's a lawyer here in Acorn Falls, but he still does a lot of work with people out on the reservation.

I looked at my father in exasperation. "Dad! Will you make Charlie settle down and finish his breakfast?"

"Charlie!" my father called, walking toward the den. "Be a good boy and do what your sister tells you. You know Mommy isn't feeling well."

With that, he pulled on his gray trenchcoat, tucked his briefcase under one arm, said, "Have a good day, honey," and was out the door.

That wasn't much help, I thought miserably. Then I glanced at the kitchen clock. 8:05! If I didn't hurry and get Charlie ready, he was going to miss his school bus.

"Okay, Charlie," I called, walking into the den, "time to get your sneakers on."

Just then I heard a crash from the living room. "Charlie, are you all right?" I called, hurrying through the den and into the living room.

But when I got to the living room, Charlie was

nowhere in sight. One of my mother's plants lay on the wooden floor. The clay pot was cracked in half and lay in a big mound of dirt.

"Oh, no," I said, bending over and trying to scoop some of the dirt back into the cracked pot. My mother wasn't going to be very happy about this. Here I was, supposed to be supervising Charlie, and I had let him knock over one of her plants.

My mother loves plants. I guess you could say she has a green thumb. Our whole living room is filled with plants — there are plants in baskets hanging in front of the bay window, plants in pots all over the oak coffee table and end tables, and potted trees on the floor. We also have a garden on the side of the house, and you can see the flowers and vines through the paned glass windows of the dining room. One thing I really like about our house is all the windows. It makes me feel like I'm always outdoors.

Now I could hear Charlie running around upstairs. I realized I'd better save cleaning up the plant for later and concentrate on getting Charlie ready for school before his school bus arrived or he got my mother out of bed.

I climbed the stairs two at a time, which

wasn't too hard, with my long legs. At five foot seven, I'm taller than most of my friends. It used to bother me, but now I'm kind of getting used to it — which is probably good, since I'm not showing any signs of getting shorter.

"Charlie . . ." I whispered, tiptoeing down the hall past my parents' room. "Charlie . . ."

Just then Charlie popped out of the linen closet. His cardboard race car was gone, and he had a blue flowered sheet over his head.

"Boo!" he yelled. "I'm a ghost!"

"Sssshhh," I told him. "You'll wake Mom."

"Ghosts don't have moms."

"Sure they do," I answered, "especially blue flowered ghosts. But sometimes blue flowered ghosts have to remember to be quiet and let their moms rest." I felt for his hand beneath the sheet and led him into his room. "Now let's go find your sneakers."

"Ghosts don't have sneakers," he told me.

I sighed. Charlie can be a lot of fun, but sometimes he's kind of hard to handle. And lately, with my mother spending so much time resting or getting things ready for the new baby, and my father involved in his work as usual, it seemed like I was taking care of him practically all the time.

Just as I sat Charlie down on his bed, I heard the school bus pull up in front of our house and blow the horn.

"Come on, Charlie, we've got to hurry!" I took the sheet off his head and began feeling under the bed for his sneakers. There was a ton of stuff under there. I pulled out three plastic soldiers, a yo-yo with no string, thousands of other plastic soldiers, and a shoe box full of rocks before I finally found his sneakers.

Sometimes it's amazing to think that Charlie and I are related. Sure, we both have the same straight, thick black hair, and my father says we both have my mother's eyes, but our personalities are really different. Charlie's kind of wild, and he always seems to be in a hurry, which is probably why his room is such a mess. I'm just the opposite, though. I'm usually pretty organized, and I like to take time to think things out before I do them. I couldn't help wondering what my new little brother or sister would be like.

I quickly stuck Charlie's sneakers on his feet and laced them up. The bus driver honked the horn again. I raised the window and yelled that Charlie would be right down.

"Hurry, Charlie!" I cried, practically dragging him down the stairs.

"Okay, Charlie, have a good day," I said, handing him his backpack as he raced down the front steps.

Whew! I closed the front door and collapsed on the couch in the living room. Now I would have just enough time to get my own things together and ride my bike to school. Then I saw the plant on the living room floor. I had to clean it up before I left.

I scooped up the mess as fast as I could and headed into the kitchen to throw it away.

When I got into the kitchen, I glanced up at the clock above the sink. 8:25! I couldn't believe it. I had never left for school later than 8:15! I was going to have to ride pretty fast if I wanted to get there on time.

I hurried over to the kitchen counter and reached for my lunch. My grandmother makes our lunches every night. She also makes the best lunches in the entire world. There's always a sandwich on her homemade bread, and usually freshly baked cookies, too. Suddenly I noticed another bag on the counter.

"Oh, no," I said. "Charlie forgot his lunch!"

I realized I'd have to drop Charlie's lunch off on my way to school even though it meant riding eight blocks out of my way on my bike to stop at Acorn Grammar before heading to Bradley Junior High.

I definitely wasn't going to make it to school on time. But I couldn't stand to think of Charlie opening up his backpack at lunchtime and not finding his lunch. Besides, I didn't think my mother would be too happy about it either.

I grabbed my things and ran out the house and hopped on my bike. I rode as fast as I could, but by the time I dropped off Charlie's lunch and got to Bradley Junior High, I was twenty minutes late to school. And by the time I stopped in at the administration office to get a late pass, then went to my locker to put away my jean jacket and get my books, I had missed first period completely.

Chapter Two

I couldn't believe it. I'm never late for school, and I had never missed first period before. I'm one of those people who almost always arrive early for everything. Somehow it makes me feel more organized if I have time to check my schedule and make sure I have everything I need in my book bag before the day begins.

I also like to get to school early so I have plenty of time to talk to my three best friends, Katie Campbell, Sabrina Wells, and Randy Zak. The four of us usually meet near our lockers when we get to school. I knew they must have wondered where I was this morning, especially when they knew my mom was so close to having her baby.

I tried not to let it bother me, but I couldn't get rid of the feeling that I was still rushing to catch up to the rest of the day. I didn't even get to talk to Katie, Sabs, and Randy until lunchtime.

I found Katie and Sabrina sitting together at a table in the corner.

"Hi," I sighed, sliding into the empty space next to Katie and putting down my lunch bag.

"Allison! Where were you this morning?" Sabrina burst out. Her hazel eyes looked like they were about to pop out of her head. She was wearing a hot pink turtleneck that matched the two bright spots on her cheeks exactly.

"Is everything okay?" asked Katie, tucking her blond hair behind her ears and looking concerned.

I sighed. "Things were really busy at home," I explained. "I just couldn't seem to get out of the house on time."

"Now you sound like me!" said Sabrina, laughing. Sabs is always saying that she's late due to reasons beyond her control, and I have to admit, I was beginning to understand what she meant.

Just then Randy walked over with her lunch tray and put it down next to Sabrina. As usual, Randy had on a really amazing outfit. Randy used to live in New York City, and she's a pretty wild dresser. Today she was wearing an oversized white T-shirt, black-and-white-checked leggings, and her black lace-up boots. On her left wrist were about ten snap bracelets, all in different patterns of black-and-white.

"Hi, Randy," I said, smiling.

Randy grinned. "I think we'd definitely better call the newspapers about this one. I can see the headlines now: ALLISON CLOUD, LATE FOR SCHOOL."

Sabrina giggled.

"I know, I know," I said, resting my head on my hand, "but I couldn't help it. My mother was resting, and I was supposed to get Charlie ready for school. But first he wouldn't eat his breakfast. *Then* he knocked over a plant, *then* I couldn't find his sneakers, *then* he almost missed his bus, *then* I forgot to put his lunch in his backpack, and *then* I had to ride over to the elementary school and drop it off!"

"Wow," said Randy, "sounds like you had your hands full."

"Yeah, this new baby is sure changing things at our house." I sighed.

"I know what that's like," said Katie, taking a bite of her apple. "When my mother was planning her wedding to Jean-Paul, things were really busy at my house. For a while it seemed like my family only noticed I was there when they needed me to run an errand or something.

And then after my mother and Jean-Paul got back from their honeymoon, we had to pack up everything in our old house and move. I was so busy just trying to keep up with it all that half the time I didn't have time to think."

I smiled at Katie. I knew it hadn't been easy for her when her mother remarried. Suddenly she not only got a new stepfather, but a new stepbrother and a new home, too. It was nice, though, in a way, to know that I wasn't the only one trying to get used to something new.

"Hey," said Sabs, "speaking of moving, have you come up with any ideas for your new room yet, Allison?"

It was just like Sabs to think of the bright side. I couldn't believe I had completely forgotten about my new room. Since my bedroom was right next to my parents', they had decided that the new baby should move in there. I was supposed to get a brand-new room, which was going to be built on top of my grandparents' addition in the back of the house.

"Didn't you say they were going to start building it soon?" asked Randy.

"That's right!" I said. "My father told me last night that the builders were going to start sometime this week." I wondered if the builders were at my house at that very moment.

"Well, then, we have to get started!" exclaimed Sabrina happily, her auburn curls bouncing up and down.

I looked at her. "Started?" I asked. Did Sabs think we were going to build my new room?

"Started doing what?" asked Katie.

"Why, planning the decor, of course!" Sabs answered. "Didn't you say that your parents were going to let you get some new stuff for your room?"

"Well, my mother did mention something about getting a new bedspread and curtains. And of course it'll need to be painted. But everything's been so busy at home lately that I haven't really had time to think about it."

"Well, then, it's time to start thinking about it now," said Sabrina happily. "The most important thing is choosing the mood of the room."

"Oh, no!" groaned Randy. "She sounds like that woman who decorated your new house, Katie. What was her name again?"

"Mrs. Gold," said Katie, wrinkling her nose. "The one who wanted me to have that 'seafoam-green' carpeting."

"Mold-green was more like it," Sabrina joked.

I laughed, remembering the flashy decorator who had thought her ideas about how to decorate Katie's room were more important than Katie's own ideas.

"No, really," insisted Sabs. "You can do a really good job if you decorate it yourself. But you do have to know a few things about which colors create which moods. I read a great article in *Young Chic* all about decorating."

I looked at Randy. She had this big grin and a you-know-Sabrina look on her face. Katie looked at me and just shrugged her shoulders. Sabrina collects tons of magazines, and she's always telling us about articles she's read.

"I don't know, Sabs," I said. "I mean, the room isn't even built yet."

"Well, this way we can have it all planned out, and you'll be ready to decorate it as soon as it's finished," she said.

"That makes sense," said Katie.

"Maybe you're right," I said. "I guess it would be fun to plan some changes."

"Sounds cool," said Randy.

"I've got a great idea," said Katie. "Let's

have a sleepover at my house on Friday. I'm
sure my mom will say it's okay. Then Sabs can
bring the magazine article and we can all help
Allison plan her new room. And of course"—
she paused to look at Sabrina — "find just the
right mood." Katie started waving her hand
around like Mrs. Gold, and we all burst out
laughing.

"That sounds great," I said when I finally
managed to catch my breath. I had laughed so
hard I was starting to feel sick. But it did sound
great. Spending some time with my very best
friends was just what I needed.

Chapter Three

After school I practically flew home on my bicycle. It had rained during the afternoon, and I had to ride around the puddles to keep from getting splashed.

I had been thinking about Sabrina's plan to redecorate my new room. Even though my father said the builders were starting sometime in the week, I really hoped it would be today. I was really excited to see if the builders had come. So when I got home, instead of going straight in the front door like I usually do, I leaned my bike against the side of the house and walked around to the back to take a look.

To my disappointment, there were no workers there at all. In fact, things looked almost the same as they had that morning. There was a box of tools on the back porch, and a couple of pieces of wood leaning up against the side of my grandparents' room, but that was it.

I pulled open the back door and stepped into the kitchen.

"Hello?" I called out. "Mom? Nooma?"

Nooma is what we call my grandmother. It comes from the Chippewa word for grandmother.

"We're in here," my mother's voice called out from the storage room next to the kitchen.

I opened the door and found my mother and Nooma sitting inside sorting through a box of baby clothes.

"Hi, sweetie," said my mother. "How was school?"

"Hi," I said. "School was all right. Katie invited me to a sleepover at her house on Friday. Can I go?"

"That sounds fine, Allison," said my mother, peering at a red baby sweater with a blue sailboat on the front that had once been Charlie's.

"Nooma, what do you think of this?" she asked, holding up the sweater for my grandmother to see. "There's a little rip in the elbow, but otherwise it seems fine, don't you think?"

My grandmother took the sweater from her. "I think we can repair it," she said, examining the sleeve.

"Mom?" I said. "Can I ask you something?"

"Sure, dear, what is it?" said my mother, brushing the lint off a yellow baby blanket.

"Have the builders called to say when they're going to start on my room?"

"Yes, as a matter of fact, they have. They're going to start on Wednesday," she said, putting the blanket down on the chair next to her. "The foreman did come over this morning to confirm some of the details."

My grandmother held up a tiny white sun hat for my mother to see. "What do you think, Meredith? This will be useful, won't it?"

"Oh, yes," said my mother. "Put it on that pile over there, would you, Nooma?" I tried not to seem too disappointed. I knew it was no big deal that the builders were going to start Wednesday instead of today. But somehow I couldn't help feeling like my new room was the last thing on my mother's mind. It seemed like lately all anyone in my family had time to think about was the new baby.

"I think I'll get some cookies and go up to my room for a while," I said. I knew I would feel better once I was relaxing in my window seat with a book.

"Oh, honey, would you keep an eye on Charlie?" asked my mother. "He's outside in his tree house. Your grandfather went to visit a sick friend and won't be back until dinnertime."

"But, Mom, I —" Then I stopped. I decided it was easier just to watch Charlie than to get into a big argument about it, so I smiled and said, "Sure, Mom."

I walked back inside and grabbed some of Nooma's homemade oatmeal cookies from the cookie jar in the kitchen. Then I headed out the back door and walked around the side of the house toward Charlie's tree house.

"Take that!" he yelled. "Take that, you enemy spy!" A stick came flying out of the tree house and landed on the ground.

I sat down on the grass with a sigh. I didn't mind watching Charlie, I just didn't feel like watching him *right now.* I thought of my cozy window seat waiting upstairs, and all of a sudden I couldn't help feeling kind of mad.

All I wanted was a little time to myself, and here I was, taking care of Charlie again. It was starting to seem like all I ever did was baby-sit. And it didn't look like things would be getting any easier. After all, soon I was going to have another little brother or sister to take care of. I guessed I was just going to have to get used to it.

I ended up taking care of Charlie for the rest of the afternoon. Soon my father came home, and it was time for dinner.

We were all sitting at the table eating my grandmother's spiced chicken with rice when my mother started to talk about an advertisement she'd seen for a baby store called Bundle of Joy in the Widmere Mall.

"They're going out of business on Saturday, and they're keeping the store open late Friday night for a one-night-only sale," she explained. "They have everything we need for the new baby."

"Baby, baby, stick your head in gravy!" Charlie sang out, his mouth full of chicken.

My father wrinkled his forehead. "Sounds great, Meredith," he said, serving himself some more rice.

A few minutes later my father said, "Oh, no, I can't go with you Friday. I just remembered I have a late meeting at the office with an important client. I don't think I'll be home until around nine o'clock."

"Well, I guess I can take Nooma with me,"

said my mother. "And if we buy anything really big, we can have it delivered."

"Oh, Meredith," my grandmother said, "remember your father and I were invited out that evening. Maybe I should cancel . . . but we were planning to see people we haven't seen in a long time," said Nooma.

"It's all right, Mother, keep your plans. We'll figure something out." My mother smiled and patted my grandmother's hand.

I cleared my throat. "Don't forget, Mom, I'm supposed to sleep over at Katie's on Friday," I said.

My father looked up from his plate. "Then who's going to take care of your brother?" he asked.

"Oh, Allison," said my mother, "it would really be a big help to me to have you stay home and look after Charlie that night."

I couldn't believe it! After all the time I had spent taking care of Charlie lately, now they wanted me to miss Katie's sleepover so I could baby-sit again.

"Can't you and Nooma go to the store during the day?" I asked quietly.

My mother was quiet for a moment. Then

she said, "I'm sorry, Al, but I have to take my car to the mechanic that day. I'm dropping it off around eight in the morning and I won't get it back until six. As it is, we've already had to wait two weeks for the appointment. And after the baby comes, I won't be able to put the car in for several more weeks."

"But, Mom, you said I could go to Katie's," I pointed out.

"Well, I didn't realize we had so much going on," said my mother. "I don't have much of a choice. The sale's only on for that one night."

I could feel my face getting warm.

"Allison, you can see your friends anytime at all," said my father. "Your mother needs you to help out that night."

"But you don't understand," I said, feeling tears suddenly burning in my eyes. "Katie practically arranged the whole thing because of me, so we could all talk about ideas for decorating my new room."

"Well, there's plenty of time for that," said my grandmother.

"Yes," said my father, "the builders haven't even started yet. You'll just have to reschedule with your friends."

"But it's not fair," I said, blinking furiously to keep back the tears.

My father looked at me sternly. "I'm sorry, Allison, but that's it. You know the family is counting on you to take care of your brother."

Before I knew what was happening, I was standing up. I could feel the tears about to spill out of my eyes and roll down my cheeks.

"Well, I'm getting sick and tired of everyone counting on me!" I yelled. "From now on, you can all count me out!"

I turned from the table and ran out of the dining room and up the stairs as fast as I could. Slamming the door of my room behind me, I threw myself down on my bed and cried until I felt like there weren't any tears left inside me.

A little while later, I wiped my face, blew my nose, and sat in my window seat looking out at the stars. I couldn't help thinking about how much I was going to miss my window seat when I moved to the new room. This was where I wrote my poetry, and it was my favorite spot to curl up with a good book. Suddenly it seemed like so many things were changing at once, and I couldn't help wishing that somehow everything could just stay the same.

My parents were probably mad at me for yelling and storming off like that. I had never really done anything like it before, and I knew they must have been really shocked. Matter of fact, the more I thought about it, though, the more I realized that I was probably most surprised of all.

Chapter Four

"Allison, there you are!" cried Sabrina, hurrying over to my locker the next morning. "I didn't see you get in."

"Oh, hi, Sabs," I said and reached into my locker for my history book. I was still feeling sort of upset about what had happened with my parents the night before, and I definitely wasn't looking forward to telling Sabs, Katie, and Randy that I couldn't come to the sleepover on Friday.

"Wait till you see what I've been doing!" Sabs said happily, taking hold of my arm and pulling me toward her locker.

Katie, who shares a locker with Sabrina, was already there, taking off her jacket, smoothing down her navy miniskirt with the wide belt, and tucking in her white blouse. I noticed that she was wearing navy tights and flats that matched her skirt exactly. Her blond ponytail was tied with a navy-and-white-striped ribbon.

"Hi, Allison," said Katie. "I guess Sabrina's already told you about her notebook. I think it's a pretty good idea, don't you?"

I looked at Sabs. "What notebook?" I asked.

"That's what I wanted to show you!" said Sabs happily. "It's right here in my schoolbag."

Sabrina reached into her half of the locker and tugged at her blue flowered backpack.

"It's right in here." Sabs grunted, pulling at the backpack, which seemed to be stuck in the locker. "If I could just get . . . this . . . thing . . . out . . ."

Suddenly the backpack came flying out of the locker, bringing several books and loose papers with it. Sabrina, who had been leaning backward in order to pull it, ended up sitting on the floor with the bag on her lap.

"There," she said, grinning. "I have to remember to add 'reorganize locker' to my list of things to do this week."

I looked at Katie, who was smiling. Sabs loves making lists, but sometimes she's better at writing things down than she is at getting them done. She had been saying she was going to clean out her part of the locker since the beginning of the year.

"Well," said Sabs, who had been digging through her schoolbag, "here it is!" In her hand she held a purple loose-leaf notebook.

"What is it?" I asked.

"It's a decorator's notebook," answered Sabs. "Actually, it's my loose-leaf notebook from last year. But as far as we're concerned, it's a decorator's notebook. All the big-name interior designers use them. It's for your new room."

"Sabs, I have plenty of notebooks already," I said, laughing.

"I know that," she said. "This is for Friday night at Katie's." She opened the notebook and began turning the pages. "See, this section here has all the articles I could find in my magazines on redecorating a bedroom. And this here's where we write down any ideas we think of."

I could feel my stomach sinking. How could I tell them that I couldn't come on Friday, especially now that Sabs had done all that work?

"Now," Sabrina went on, "one thing you should start thinking about is your color scheme. You know, what color you want to paint the walls and stuff."

"But, Sabs —" I began.

"No, really," she interrupted. "Color scheme is

important. It can make or break your room."

"Hey," said Katie, "I just thought of something. My mother has some booklets of paint samples left over from when she and Mrs. Gold picked the colors for our new house. I'm sure she'd let us have them."

"Great," said Sabs. "We can cut out all the ones we think are possibilities for Allison's room and paste them into the notebook."

"Oh, and my mom said we can make brownies if we want," said Katie.

"Listen," I broke in, "I have to tell you guys something I —"

But suddenly I was cut off by Randy, who had just arrived.

"Hi, everyone," she said, pulling off her black leather jacket and slinging it over her shoulder. "What's up?"

"It's about Friday night," I began.

"Oh, yeah," said Randy, "that reminds me. There's this really great horror flick on TV on Friday night — *Horror High School*. We should all definitely watch it at your house, Katie."

"Randy, we're supposed to be having this sleepover to work on the design for Allison's new room," Sabrina reminded her.

"We can still work on it," Randy answered, "between murders!" She put both hands around her neck, stuck out her tongue, and crossed her eyes.

"Listen, everyone," I began again, "that's just what I want to talk to you about —"

"Don't worry, Allison, we can work on your room before the movie starts," said Sabs.

"But —" I tried to say something again. But I was cut off by the bell.

"I've got to run," said Sabs, throwing her backpack into her locker and tucking her clarinet case under one arm. "I have band practice."

"Come on, Katie," said Randy. "We have math, and I can't be late again, or Miss Munson will eat me alive. Grrrrrr!" she growled, letting her eyes bulge and baring her teeth. "If they ever make a movie called *Horror at Bradley Junior High*, she could play the monster."

Before I knew it, everyone was rushing off toward their classes. And even though I hadn't had a chance to tell Randy, Katie, and Sabs about Friday night, I knew I'd better hurry, too. I didn't want to be late for first-period history class.

First period flew by and then it was time for my second period. Instead of a regular class, I had a special tutoring session with Billy Dixon. I met Billy a few months earlier when I volunteered to be a peer tutor.

Peer tutors are supposed to help students who are having trouble with their schoolwork. It sounded like a great idea, but when Billy and I first started working together, we had a really tough time. He seemed so smart in some ways, but some things were really difficult for him, especially reading. And he didn't exactly appreciate my trying to help him. But eventually we learned to get along, and now we're really good friends.

It turned out that the reason Billy had so much trouble in school was that he was dyslexic, which is a reading problem where you see letters and words backward. Since then, along with our tutoring session, he's been going to a reading specialist every day.

After Billy and I got used to working together, we decided to turn our once-a-week tutoring period into a study session. It's a great chance for us to go over some of the work that we each have from other classes. It's fun, and we learn that much more.

I found Billy sitting in the classroom where

we usually meet with his feet on the desk in front of him and an open book across his lap. He was wearing a pair of worn jeans and a blue T-shirt, and he was gazing out the window toward the empty soccer field.

"Hi," I said, putting my books down on the desk next to his.

"Oh, hi, Allison," he said, jumping a little. "I didn't hear you come in."

"It's starting to feel like no one *ever* hears me," I said to myself, thinking how hard it had been to get people to listen to me lately.

Billy took his feet off the desk and turned to face me.

"What do you mean?" he asked, looking at me with a concerned expression in his deep blue eyes.

"Oh, it's nothing," I said. "Nothing important."

Billy looked at me again.

"Are you sure, Allison?" he asked.

"Really," I said, taking a deep breath and opening my notebook. "Let's just forget about it and get to work. Did you read the poem for English yet?"

Billy took the book off his lap.

31

"Well," he said, opening it on the desk, "I tried. But I just can't seem to get into it. I mean, I understand the words and everything, but I just don't get the point. I mean, what's it supposed to be about?"

I picked up the book and looked at the poem. It was a sonnet by Elizabeth Barrett Browning, who is one of my favorite poets, so I knew it well.

"Well, first of all, it's a love poem," I explained. "Elizabeth Barrett Browning wrote a whole bunch of them for her husband, Robert Browning."

"Yeah," Billy said, shaking a lock of his dark hair off his forehead, "it seemed kind of mushy and sentimental."

"It also helps if you know something about Elizabeth Barrett Browning," I told him. "I read a book about her last summer. She wrote her first book of poetry when she was just thirteen, when her name was still Elizabeth Barrett."

"Wow," said Billy. "She sounds like you, Allison."

I felt my face flush. I've been writing poems for a while, and I've even read a couple of them to Billy. It made me feel really good to hear him compare me to a real poet.

"So then when did this Browning guy come into the picture?" asked Billy.

"Not until much later," I told him. "You see, Elizabeth Barrett had a pretty lonely life at first. I guess that's one reason she wrote poetry. Then one day Robert Browning, who was also a poet, wrote her a fan letter. Elizabeth Barrett wrote back to him, and for years the two of them kept writing each other letters filled with poetry, until they finally got married."

"That's a cool story," said Billy, picking up the book and looking at it again. "It kind of gives the poem more meaning."

"Another thing that can make it more meaningful is reading it out loud," I told him. "Whenever I have trouble understanding a poem, I read it out loud to myself."

"I find a lot of things easier to understand if someone reads them out loud," said Billy quietly. I knew he meant that he sometimes had trouble reading silently to himself because of his dyslexia.

"Well, with poetry it's especially important," I told him. "That way you can really hear the rhythm of the words."

"Allison? Can I ask you to do something?" asked Billy in a low voice.

"Sure, Billy," I said. "What is it?"

"Do you think you could read this poem out loud to me? I think it would really help."

At first I felt kind of shy about doing it, but then I decided that Billy was right. It would probably help both of us understand the poem if I read it out loud.

"Okay," I said, taking the book from him.

When I first began reading, I still felt a little embarrassed, especially since it was a love poem. But the words were really beautiful, and as I went on, I became more and more involved in them.

Just as I finished, the bell rang.

I put down the book and saw Billy looking at me. His blue eyes were shining.

"That was beautiful, Allison," he said. "Thank you."

"Thank you, Billy," I answered. And I meant it. Somehow, reading the poem had calmed me. For the first time since my blowup at the dinner table the night before, I actually felt happy.

And it turned out to be a good idea for another reason, too. Billy and I had next period

together, which was English and also homeroom. During English class, Ms. Staats assigned
an essay on the Elizabeth Barrett Browning
poem, due next week. When she made the
announcement, Billy turned to me and winked.

After English class and a few homeroom
announcements, it was time for lunch. I had to
stop by my locker to get a few books for my
afternoon classes, so I told Katie, Sabs, and
Randy that I'd meet them in the cafeteria.

By the time we all met in the cafeteria and
found a table, Sabs was in the middle of telling
us about a movie she'd seen the night before. I
swear, Sabs is the only person I know who
remembers every single line of every single
movie she's ever seen.

As lunch went on, we were all having such a
good time that I didn't feel like talking about
the fight I'd had with my parents and why I
couldn't come over Friday night. I was still disappointed about it, but somehow I didn't feel
quite as angry. I know it's funny, but somehow
being with my very best friends had helped. I
figured I would just call everyone after school
and tell them all about it.

Chapter Five

The rest of the day flew by, and before I knew it, school was over. I felt a little funny about facing my mother. I had kept expecting my parents to come up to my room after what happened. But the next thing I knew, I had awakened in the middle of the night with a blanket over me and the lights turned out in my room. I guess my parents figured I needed some time alone after my outburst.

When I got up for school in the morning, Mom was still in bed. Dad had laid out everything for our breakfast and a note that just said he'd be home in time for dinner. Surprisingly, Charlie was as good as gold, and I had no trouble getting him off to school. He made the school bus on time, and I remembered to put his lunch in his backpack.

But now it was time to go home, and I couldn't help wondering if my mother would still be angry with me. I knew I was going to have a lot of explaining to do.

The first thing I noticed as I rode my bike up our driveway was the noise coming from behind the house. There was the sound of hammering and sawing, and suddenly I realized that the builders must be back there working on my new room!

I leaned my bike against the house and hurried around the back. There was my mother, standing on the back porch, looking up at two men who were hammering boards into the roof of my grandparents' room. A third man was cutting wood planks with an electric saw in the backyard.

Just then my mother turned around and saw me. She gave me a big smile and waved. Then she motioned for me to follow her inside.

Once inside the kitchen, she turned to me.

"Well, the builders started a day early. I have a good feeling about your new room, Allison." Then she looked serious. "There are a couple of things I want to talk to you about."

I took a deep breath. I was sure she wanted to talk to me about last night, and I didn't think it was going to be good.

"Your grandfather took Charlie for a walk, and Nooma's making dinner, so we have plenty of time to ourselves. Let's make a snack and go sit in the den where it's quiet," she said.

I was surprised. I haven't made my parents mad very often, but even when I have, Mom had never suggested we have a snack before she started talking to me. I couldn't help feeling like it was my last meal or something.

Nooma looked up and smiled when we walked into the kitchen. She seemed really busy with whatever she was making and turned her attention back to her mixing bowls and cookbook.

My mother cut two slices of the pecan bread my grandmother had baked, and spread cream cheese on them, while I poured two glasses of orange juice. We carried our plates and glasses into the den and sat down on the dark red paisley-print sofa. The den is right under my room, in the front of the house, and it has a big curved window like the one in my room. The only difference is that my window has a window seat built into the curve, and the window in the den has an open space that the sofa fits into. One thing I love about both places is that when you sit in the window seat or the sofa, you can see through the windows around you on three sides. It almost feels like you're sitting outside.

"Well, Allison," said my mother, putting her plate down on the low coffee table in front of her, "I really wanted to talk to you about what happened last night."

"I thought so," I mumbled, looking down at my lap and nibbling on a corner of my pecan bread.

"I understand why you were upset," she said. "I've been so busy with plans for the new baby that I think I've just taken it for granted you would be around to take care of Charlie whenever I wanted. Also, it was wrong of me to tell you that you couldn't go to Katie's after I had already said it was okay."

I looked at her in surprise.

"I've arranged for Charlie to spend Friday night with one of his friends from school. That way everyone can keep their plans, and I can go shopping in peace."

"Oh, Mom," I said, "are you sure?"

"Positive," she said. "I told you that you could go to Katie's, and it's not right for me to go back on my word. Besides, you could probably use a little break from all the baby-sitting you've been doing. I know Charlie can be a lot to handle."

Fantastic! Now I didn't have to call Katie, Sabs, and Randy and cancel after all.

"But, Al," my mother continued, "you have to do something for me."

"Anything you want, Mom," I answered happily.

"Well, when the baby comes, you've got to help Nooma around the house and with Charlie as much as you can. I will probably be back on my feet after a couple of weeks."

"You've got a deal, Mom. And . . . Mom . . ." I said, turning to look at her, "I'm sorry about what I said last night. I really didn't mean it. I guess I was just upset."

"I know, honey. There's a lot going on around here. But you're doing a great job, and I appreciate your help." Then my mother reached over and gave me a hug. It was a little awkward because of the baby. Suddenly the baby gave a big kick, and we started laughing because it seemed like it was saying, "Hey, what about me!"

"Now let's talk about your new room," my mother continued after taking a sip of her juice.

"I saw the builders out back," I said, picking up my glass of juice. "Is everything going okay?"

"Oh, sure," she answered. "They're just starting on the basic frame. When they get that done, they're going to cut a place in the upstairs hallway for a door leading from the hallway into your new room. The door to your room will end up being right next to the door to your father's study. Meanwhile, what you and I need to figure out now is where you want the windows."

She stood up and walked over to the antique desk in the corner.

"Come and look at the plans for the room," she said, looking down at a pile of papers on the desk. "See, these are the four walls. One is the wall with the door in it, which is where your room is attached to the rest of the house. That leaves us three possible walls for windows."

She spread the papers out on the desk in front of us. At first the drawings were a little hard for me to figure out, but then I realized that they were pretty much like maps, except that instead of showing the borders of different countries, they showed the borders of my new room.

"This side here faces the side of the house where the big chestnut tree with Charlie's tree house is," said my mother, pointing at one of the walls in the drawings. "This wall on the opposite side faces the garden, and the one in between looks out on the backyard. It all depends which view you like the best."

I studied the drawings. It was really hard to decide where the windows should go. I liked all three views. Suddenly I had an idea.

"Mom, do you think I could have windows on all three sides?" I asked.

My mother's face brightened.

"What a wonderful idea, Allison!" she said. "With windows stretching across all three walls, it will be bright and sunny during the day, and at night you'll be able to see the stars."

"That sounds really nice," I said excitedly. "Almost like being outside."

Suddenly my mother raised her eyebrows.

"That gives me another idea," she said, bending over to look at the plans. "Yes, that's it. That's it. Look here." She pointed to the drawing of the wall that faced the garden. "How about if we have this wall built farther back into the room a few feet? That way we can turn the extra space into a little terrace overlooking the garden — and you can go outside whenever you want to."

"That's a great idea!" I exclaimed. Imagine, my own private terrace. It made me feel like Juliet in the play *Romeo and Juliet.*

"We'll have them put a french door in that wall, too, so it will be really romantic," she said, smiling at me. "And maybe some stairs from the terrace down to the backyard so you can use the terrace as a second entrance to your room."

"Oh, Mom, I love it!" I said happily, moving over on the couch to give her a hug. "It's perfect!"

I couldn't believe it. Suddenly it was starting to sound like my new room was going to be the most special place in the whole house.

Chapter Six

I stood in front of the huge wooden front door to Katie's house and pressed the bell, and listened to the chimes ringing somewhere inside. I had to admit, I still wasn't completely used to Katie's new house. Katie and her stepfather, Jean-Paul Beauvais, her mother, her sister, Emily, and her stepbrother, Michel, had moved into it only a few weeks ago. It's really enormous, bigger than any house I've ever been inside, and the grounds seem to go on forever and ever.

A few moments later, the door was opened by the housekeeper. That's another thing that's kind of hard to get used to. Katie's family has three servants now, the housekeeper, a cook, and a groundskeeper who lives in an apartment over the garage. Although the other servants don't live with them, the housekeeper and cook are usually there until about seven in the evening because Katie's mom and Mr. Beauvais usually work late.

"Hello, miss," said the housekeeper, stepping back and showing me into the huge entry hall. "Miss Katie and her friend are in the back, at the tennis courts. You can go straight out, if you like."

"Thanks," I mumbled, heading down the hall. My shoes clicked on the polished wood floors as I passed the living room, the dining room, the study, and a bunch of other rooms I couldn't even identify. It was amazing how empty a house this big could seem, even with five family members and three servants. I thought of my own busy house and smiled to myself.

As I stepped out onto the slate patio, I could hear voices and the sound of tennis rackets smashing against balls echoing over the grounds. I made my way down the stone path to the tennis courts, where I could see Katie with a tennis racket in her hand. She was wearing a white sweatshirt and white sweatpants, and on her feet were a pair of white tennis shoes.

On the other side of the net was Randy, who had on a pair of black leggings with bright green high-top sneakers and a black-and-white-striped turtleneck. She wore her black leather jacket, and on her head was a bright-green-and-black bicycle cap.

"Take that, you tennis ball!" yelled Randy, swinging her racket and smashing the ball over the net to Katie.

"You're getting much better, Randy!" called Katie, easily returning the ball with her racket. She turned her head and saw me standing just outside the court. "Oh, hi, Allison," she said. "I was just giving Randy a tennis lesson. Not that she really needs it. I think she might just be a natural at this."

"Hi, Al!" called Randy, jumping over the net with the racket in her hand. "You should try this, it's fun. It kind of reminds me of playing handball in Central Park with Sheck."

Sheck is Randy's best friend in New York City. She talks about him all the time. We all finally got to meet him when he came to Acorn Falls for a visit over Thanksgiving. He's really cute and seems like a real nice guy.

"It's getting kind of cold out here. Let's all go back to the house and have a snack or something," suggested Katie. "Besides, Sabs should be here any minute."

"I didn't know you played tennis," I said to Katie on our way back to the house.

"Actually, I'm still learning," she told me.

"Jean-Paul has arranged for me and Michel to take lessons at the country club when it gets warmer. You should see how good Michel is, though. He started taking lessons back in Canada when he was only seven."

"No problem," joked Randy. "Let me at him. I'll show him how the game is played."

"Where is Michel, anyway?" I asked.

"Oh, he's up in his room, trying to finish this book so he can write a book report on it for Monday," said Katie, leading the way into the house.

"Really? The report's due Monday, and he hasn't even finished the book yet?" I asked. I couldn't imagine leaving my work till the last minute like that.

Katie shrugged. "Michel's not exactly the organized type," she pointed out.

A few minutes later we were sitting up in Katie's room with a big bowl of fruit, some popcorn, and some sodas.

"Cook said not to eat anything too heavy, because she's making our dinner now," Katie explained. "My mother and Jean-Paul are going out, and Emily has a date with her boyfriend, so it's just going to be the four of us and Michel."

"Speaking of the four of us, where's Sabs?" asked Randy.

"Yeah, shouldn't she be here by now?" I wondered.

"She said she was coming," said Katie, shrugging.

Just then the door to Katie's room opened and Sabrina practically fell inside.

"Hey, Sabs!" said Randy. "Finally! Are you all right?"

"Wow," Sabrina panted. "Those stairs are really something. I can't believe I finally made it. I think you should turn the elevator on when we come over."

The other totally cool thing about Katie's house is that they have an elevator in the house. The problem is it's really old, and Mr. Beauvais won't let anyone use it until he gets it fixed. But Katie suspects he doesn't really want anyone to use it because he never seems to get around to getting it fixed. We took a look at it once, though, and it really is cool. It has to be turned on with a key.

"I know," said Katie. "Jean-Paul just keeps saying that he'll call the guy next week. It's always next week. *Mon Dieu!*"

With that we started laughing because Mr. Beauvais always says *"Mon Dieu!"* and Katie can imitate him pretty well.

When we all managed to stop laughing, I asked Sabrina, "Where have you been?" I guess secretly I was kind of anxious to start talking about my new room.

"Yeah," said Randy. "You missed seeing me in action on the tennis court."

"That's not all I missed," said Sabs, sitting down on Katie's brass daybed with a sigh. "As usual, getting Luke to drive me over here was really impossible."

"What did you have to promise him this time?" asked Randy. Sabrina's always having to do things for her older brother Luke in exchange for his giving her a lift in his car to where she wants to go.

"Actually, nothing," said Sabs. "At least, not at first. Luke was in one of his incredibly rare good moods, and when I asked him to drive me, he said yes without my having to promise anything. But then he got it into his head that he knew a shortcut over here, and of course we got lost. Then he started getting really grouchy, and blaming me for the whole thing."

"That doesn't sound very fair," said Katie sympathetically.

"Well, it didn't help much when I realized I'd forgotten the decorator's notebook for Allison's room, and I had to ask him to drive me back home so I could pick it up," said Sabs.

"Wow," said Randy. "I bet Luke didn't like that one too much."

"Did you actually get him to do it?" I asked. I had to admit, I had gotten pretty excited about the whole decorating project, and I hoped Sabs had been able to bring the notebook.

"Well . . ." Sabs began.

"Here it comes," said Randy, shaking her head. "What do you have to do for Luke this time?"

"Make his bed every morning for two weeks," admitted Sabs. "But at least I got the notebook!" She reached into her orange-and-white polka-dot duffel bag and pulled out the purple notebook with a flourish.

At first I felt bad that Sabs was going to have to make Luke's bed for two weeks just because of me and my new room. But she seemed so excited about the decorating plan that I realized I would have done the same thing for her in a minute.

"Okay," said Katie, taking a bunch of grapes from the fruit bowl and sitting down on her pale blue carpeting, "so where do we start?"

"Well," said Sabs, opening the purple notebook across her lap, "according to this article from *Young Chic*, we have to figure out what kind of personality type Allison is. Then we can select the room decor that's best for her."

"That's easy," said Randy. "After all, who knows Allison better than we do?"

"Actually, there's a quiz in here that Al's supposed to take," said Sabs.

"A quiz! No problem!" said Randy. "Allison will definitely ace it."

"It's not that kind of quiz, Randy," said Sabrina. "It's more like figuring out which of the five different personality types listed is hers." She looked at me. "Are you ready, Allison?"

Ready as I'll ever be, I thought to myself. After all, how often do I get to figure out my personality type and get a new room at the same time? Only it didn't seem likely to me that there were really only five different kinds of personalities in the world, but I didn't want to tell Sabs that, not after all the trouble she had gone to. Besides I was willing to answer thousands of questions if it would help us figure out how to decorate my new room.

"Fire away," I said.

"Okay," Sabrina began, "here's the first question:

"'Your idea of a perfect place to spend a Saturday afternoon is

a) at the movies,

b) walking in the woods,

c) at a football game, or

d) in the nearest mall?'"

I didn't exactly understand what this question could have to do with my new room decor, but I decided to just answer it as honestly as I could.

"Well," I said, "I guess I'd have to say '(b), walking in the woods.' I mean, I like movies and shopping, too, but there's something really special about being outside."

"Okay," said Sabs, making a mark in her notebook. "Question number two:

"'You just won a trip to anywhere in the world for one week. Would you go to

a) Paris,

b) the Rocky Mountains,

c) China, or

d) a tropical island?'"

I had to think about that one for a moment. I knew the Rocky Mountains were probably really beautiful, but somehow I thought I'd like to go somewhere completely different.

"China," I decided.

"No fair!" said Randy. "They forgot to include New York City!"

"Randy, would you really choose New York instead of someplace you've never been?" asked Katie.

"Probably not," Randy admitted, "but I still think it should be one of the choices."

"Okay, Allison," said Sabrina, "here's question number three:

"'The outfit you feel most comfortable in is

a) a red minidress and rhinestone earrings,

b) a blazer over a plain white shirt and tailored pants,

c) a long flowered dress and a floppy straw hat, or

d) faded jeans and a really nice sweater?'"

I didn't have to give that one much thought.

"Definitely the jeans and the nice sweater," I said.

"It's kind of hard to imagine you in any of the others," Katie agreed.

"Although you'd look really great in any of them," said Sabrina.

After a few more questions, Sabs tallied up my score.

"Well," she said, "according to this, Allison, you're a 'Twilight' personality. The personalities they give are 'Dawn,' 'Daylight,' 'Sunset,' 'Twilight,' and 'Midnight.'

"It says here: 'As a Twilight person, you are down-to-earth, yet you still know how to dream. You're quiet but creative, and your surroundings are very important to you.'"

"You know," said Katie, "that does really sound like you, Allison."

I nodded. It was strange, but I had to admit, the description from the magazine seemed to fit me.

"Okay, great," said Randy. "But how does that translate into paint, curtains, and a bedspread?"

"There's more," said Sabs, picking up the notebook. "It says: 'Fill your room with the deep, rich colors of the early evening sky. Keep things simple and give your imagination somewhere to wander.'"

"The colors of the early evening sky — what do you think that means?" asked Randy.

Katie shrugged. "Blue, I guess," she said.

I closed my eyes and imagined the sky just after sunset. Twilight was one of my favorite times to be outside because of the way the sky seemed to glow.

"Purple," I said suddenly.

"What about it?" asked Sabs.

"The way the sky looks after the sun goes down," I explained. "It glows a kind of light purple color."

"Pink, too," added Sabs. "A really deep pink."

"And sort of gray-blue," Randy put in.

"I know," said Katie, jumping up. "I'll go down to the basement and get those paint samples I was telling you guys about. Then we can help Allison pick out the twilight colors she likes best."

A couple of minutes later, Katie was back with the books of paint samples. After looking through them, we decided on a pale grayish lavender for the walls and ceiling. We found a deep royal purplish blue for the woodwork and window frames that went perfectly. I decided to ask my mother for a flowered bedspread with a purple background and lavender and white flowers. Then Katie suggested sheer white curtains for the windows. By the time we were done, I felt really good about the plan for my new room.

Chapter Seven

Just then there was a knock on the door, and Katie's mother and stepfather came in to say good night before going out to dinner.

They both looked incredible. Mr. Beauvais was wearing a dark suit, and Katie's mother had on a long cream-colored dress with matching cream-colored shoes.

"We shouldn't be too late," said Katie's mother. "But don't you girls stay up too late, either."

"Cook has your dinner ready downstairs," said Katie's stepfather. "And Michel is taking a break from his studies to dine with you ladies."

"You can go ahead and make brownies if you want," said Katie's mother. "But you might want to wait until after Cook leaves tonight."

"Okay, Mom," said Katie. "Good night. Good night, Jean-Paul."

A few minutes later, Michel, Randy, Sabs, Katie, and I were all seated around the huge dining table downstairs. Since the kitchen table only fit six people, Cook decided to serve us in the dining room. I think she thought we'd be more comfortable and have more fun. But the shiny wooden dining table was so large that, even with five of us sitting there, there were big empty spaces between the place settings.

Something about sitting there in that formal dining room in those oversized chairs was really funny. Katie, Randy, Sabs, and I kept breaking out into giggles, although Michel didn't seem to think there was anything strange about it.

It was kind of weird to have the cook serve us from a tray, and I have to admit I felt sort of relieved when she left for the night. I guess I'm just not one of those people who can feel comfortable with someone waiting on them.

As we started in on our spaghetti and meatballs, I realized that I hadn't thanked my friends for helping me plan my new room.

"By the way, guys," I said, twisting some spaghetti around my fork, "I really appreciate all the help you gave me upstairs."

"No problem, Al," said Randy, popping a meatball into her mouth.

"Really," said Katie. "That's what friends are

for."

"I'm so excited, Allison," said Sabs. "I mean, I think your new room is going to be really nice."

"What is this?" asked Michel, pouring himself some more milk from the crystal pitcher on the table. "Allison is moving?"

"Well, not exactly," I said. "I mean, my family's not moving to a new house or anything. But I am getting a new bedroom."

"The new baby's going to get Allison's old room," Katie explained.

Michel's eyes lit up.

"Ah, yes," he said. "I remember this. I heard that your mother was going to be having a baby, Allison. When will the baby be born?"

"It could be any day now," I told him.

"This is very exciting!" said Michel. "And when is the party?"

I looked at Katie, who shrugged her shoulders.

"What party?" I asked Michel.

Michel looked confused. "Ah, but perhaps I am wrong," he said. "I understood that it is customary to have a party for a woman who is having a baby. You know, so that there will be many gifts waiting when the baby is born."

"Oh," said Katie. "You mean a baby shower."

Michel's face brightened. "Yes!" he said. "Yes, that is what I was thinking of."

Suddenly Sabs dropped her fork onto her plate with a clatter. "That's a great idea, Michel!" she said. "What do you think, Al?"

I looked at her. "You mean throw a baby shower for my mother?" I asked.

"Cool!" said Randy.

"That sounds like fun," said Katie.

The more I thought about it, the more I liked the idea.

"I'm sure Nooma would be willing to help with the refreshments," I said, thinking.

"I'll take care of the music," Randy volunteered.

"And we can all help you with the decorations and stuff," offered Sabs.

"I am sure the guys would be willing to pitch in as well," said Michel. "I could talk to them about it."

"Okay," I said. "But we'd better have it soon if we want to do it before the baby's born. Maybe next Saturday."

"But it should be a surprise," said Sabrina.

"I'll see if my father can get my mother out of

the house that day," I said. "And I'll make out a guest list. There'll be the five of us, Billy, Sam, Arizonna, Jason, and Nick. And of course I'll invite my mother's friends, and anyone else I can think of."

Randy's face lit up.

"We should make a big banner or something," she suggested.

"What should it say?" asked Katie.

"'Happy Baby Shower?'" Sabs tried.

Then I got an idea. "How about 'Welcome, Baby Cloud?'" I said.

"That's great," said Sabrina. "'Baby Cloud,' how cute!"

"Hey, I've got another idea," said Katie suddenly. "When I was downstairs in the basement getting the paint sample books, I found all these wallpaper samples Mrs. Gold left behind, too. Maybe we could use them to make the banner more colorful."

"Great," said Randy. "We can cut each letter out of a different wallpaper print."

"That'll look really great," said Sabs excitedly, her auburn curls bouncing.

"I think I saw an old white drop cloth we can use for the actual banner. We could glue the letters on it," said Katie.

"Okay," said Randy, picking up her plate and heading for the kitchen. "But let's hurry up and get to work. We have to be finished in forty-five minutes."

"Why?" asked Sabrina.

Randy put down her plate and pretended to be shocked.

"Don't tell me!" she said dramatically. "Don't tell me you forgot!"

"Forgot what, Randy?" asked Sabs.

"It's almost time for *Horror High School*," she said, putting her hands around her own neck and crossing her eyes.

"Eeek!" said Sabs. "Maybe I'll stay in the kitchen and make the brownies."

"I will watch the horror movie with you, Randy," volunteered Michel.

"Don't you have to finish reading that book, Michel?" asked Katie.

Michel waved his hand in the air as if he were shooing away a fly.

"If not tonight, maybe tomorrow I will finish it," he said.

I was sure Katie was going to argue with him. Katie's kind of like me about homework and getting things done, and I knew she must think it was a bad idea for Michel to put off finishing his work that way. But to my surprise, she didn't say anything.

I guess this means that Katie's starting to accept the fact that her stepbrother is very different from her, I thought. That must have been a lot for her to get used to.

Suddenly I knew I was going to have a lot of new things to get used to, too. I just hoped I was going to be able to handle it as well as Katie seemed to be doing.

Chapter Eight

"Why does Mommy have to take a shower?" Charlie asked me. "I thought she likes baths better."

I tried not to laugh. It was Sunday afternoon, and I had told Charlie to meet me up in his tree house for a secret meeting. Now I was trying to explain the plan that Sabs, Katie, Randy, and I had come up with.

"It's not that kind of shower," I explained. "The kind of shower I mean is really a party. They just call it a shower because . . . because . . ." I stopped, realizing I had no idea why it was called a shower. I would have to remember to look it up next time I was in the library.

"Can Dad come to the party, too?" asked Charlie.

"As a matter of fact, Dad's going to take Mom out somewhere that day so that we can all set up for the party. That way, when he brings Mom back to the house, she'll be surprised," I answered. I had found my father working upstairs in his study earlier that day and talked to him about the shower. He had thought it was a great idea and had promised to get my mother out of the house on Saturday.

"We have to make sure not to say anything about the party in front of Mom," I told Charlie. "Do you think you can keep it a secret?"

Charlie puffed out his chest. "I'm a spy," he told me. "Spies are really good at secrets."

"Good," I said, tousling his thick black hair. "Now, Mr. Spy, are you ready for your first assignment?"

Charlie nodded.

"Okay," I said, "Mom's in the living room with Nooma, mending baby clothes. I want you to go in and make sure she stays there while I get some phone numbers from her address book in the den."

Charlie nodded again.

"Remember," I told him, "if Mom gets up to leave the living room, you run into the den right away and tell me."

Charlie and I climbed down the rope ladder from his tree house and went into the house.

Before I went into the den, I put my hand over my mouth to remind him about the secret. He put his hand over his mouth, too, and nodded.

In the den, I opened the desk drawer where my mother keeps her address book. Pulling it out, along with a piece of notepaper and a pen, I began to look through it. I copied down the phone numbers of everyone I thought I should invite to the shower, including my mother's friends and my Aunt Pauline and Aunt Vivian. Just as I was taking one last look to make sure I hadn't left anyone out, I heard my mother's voice coming from the alcove outside the den.

"Charlie, what has gotten into you?" she was asking, and I could tell by her footsteps and the sound of her voice that she was headed right toward me.

Without thinking, I quickly shoved the address book up under my gray-and-white striped T-shirt and crumpled the paper in my hand just as Charlie burst through the doorway. He still had his hand clamped over his mouth, and his eyes looked like they were about to pop out of his head. My mother was right behind him.

"Charlie," she said with a sigh, "are you play-ing some sort of game, or what?" She looked at me. "Hi, Allison. I didn't know you were in here. Maybe you can tell me what's come over your brother. He won't take his hand off his mouth, and I can't get him to say a word."

I looked at Charlie, who was standing in the corner with his hand still over his mouth.

"That's right, Mom, it's a game," I said quickly. "A game that Charlie and I were playing before, right, Charlie?"

Charlie nodded but didn't take his hand away.

I noticed my mother looking down at my arms, which I had to keep crossed over my stomach in order to hide the bulge that the address book was making.

"Are you all right?" she asked me. "You don't have a stomach ache, do you?"

I glanced down at my folded arms.

"Oh, no," I said, trying to think of an explanation.

My mother shook her head. "Well, I don't know what's come over this family all of a sudden. Why, a little while ago, your father came downstairs from his study and announced that he was taking me to the movies next Saturday. We haven't been to a movie alone together in years!"

"That sounds nice, Mom," I said. I knew I had to get out of there before she noticed that I was hiding something under my shirt. "Come on, Charlie," I said, "let's go upstairs and finish that game."

I hurried out of the room with Charlie close behind me.

"Charlie, I didn't mean that you shouldn't say anything to Mom," I explained after we had both run up the stairs and into my room. I slipped the address book out from under my shirt and stuck it under my mattress. I would have to remember to sneak it back into the den later. "You just have to be careful not to say anything about the shower. She'll definitely know something's up if you keep acting like this until Saturday."

I sat down on my bed and started to laugh. The idea of Charlie running around all week with his hand over his mouth was pretty funny.

When Charlie saw me laughing, he started to laugh, too. Before I knew it, I was laughing so hard that I slid off the bed and down to the floor. Soon Charlie and I were both sitting on my rag rug, laughing as hard as we could.

I knew Charlie didn't even realize what it was

I had thought was so funny in the first place. But I guess that's one of the nice things about having someone younger around who's happy just to be doing what you're doing.

A few days later, Sabrina, Katie, Randy, and I all went to Party Palace after school to pick out the things we needed for the shower.

"Hey, these are really cool," said Randy, picking up a package of black plates with yellow lightning bolts on them.

"Maybe that's not really right for a baby shower," Katie suggested gently.

"Yeah, I guess you're right," said Randy. "Besides, look, the matching napkins say 'Zappy Birthday.'"

"Well, that definitely won't work, then," said Sabrina, looking through a stack of paper tablecloths. "We're not having a birthday party."

"It's almost a birthday party, though, if you think about it," I pointed out. "I mean, it's a party for someone who's about to be born."

"Oh, yeah," said Randy, "birth — day."

"Wow, Allison," said Sabs, putting down the paper tablecloth she had been looking at, "you must be so excited. I mean, any day now you're going to have another little brother or a little sister."

"Really," said Randy. "Imagine, another little Hurricane Charlie running around."

"Yeah," I said, trying to sound enthusiastic. Somehow it made me feel tired just thinking about trying to take care of two energetic little kids at the same time. But I was afraid I might sound selfish if I tried to explain, so I didn't say anything. Instead, I turned and began looking at a package of plastic forks hanging on a hook nearby.

Randy and Sabs had wandered off when I suddenly I heard Katie's voice behind me.

"Allison, is everything okay?" she asked.

I turned around to face her. I could tell by the look on her face that she knew there was something bothering me. In the next aisle I could hear Sabs and Randy blowing noisemakers.

"Well . . ." I started.

"Is it about your mother having the baby?" she asked.

"Kind of," I admitted. "But it's not that I'm not excited about the idea of having another little brother or a little sister."

"Then what is it that's bothering you?" she asked.

"It's just that I'm worried about how much

time I'm going to have to spend baby-sitting," I told her. "I mean, it's hard enough having to take care of Charlie all the time, but at least he'll be old enough soon to start taking care of himself. But I just know my parents are going to want me to help with the new baby, too."

"I see what you mean," said Katie. "I mean, I never gave it much thought before, since I was always the youngest in our family, and I never had to take care of anyone. But I guess it must be kind of hard on you."

I nodded, feeling a little lump in my throat. "I'm happy about the new baby and all. It's just that lately I feel like I'm not getting much time to myself. You know, to do the things that I like to do — reading, and writing poetry, and just being with you guys." I looked at her. "I never did get a chance to tell you this, Katie, but I almost couldn't come to your sleepover last Friday. My parents wanted me to baby-sit for Charlie instead."

"Then what happened?" she asked. "Did they change their minds?"

"My mother said she realized it wasn't fair to ask me to stay home, because she had already told me that I could go," I explained.

"Well," said Katie, "it sounds like your parents understand a little bit, then."

"Oh, I know they try, and I was definitely glad when my mother said I could come to your house," I said. "But what I'm upset about is more than just that one night. I can't help feeling like once this baby's born, I'm not going to have any free time left at all."

Katie looked at me.

"Look, Allison," she said. "I know it can be really hard to deal with big changes in your family. I went through it when my mother married Jean-Paul. But if there's one thing I learned, it's this — it's no good to just keep your feelings inside. If something is bothering you, you should talk to your parents about it."

"I don't know . . ." I said. I just wasn't used to talking to my parents about stuff like this. What if they thought I was being really selfish?

"Really," said Katie. "I mean, if you don't explain how you feel, how are they ever going to figure it out?"

Just then Sabrina and Randy came around the corner into our aisle.

"Hey, you guys!" called Randy.

"Look what we found!" said Sabs.

They hurried over to show us the paper plates

and napkins in their arms. The plates were pink and blue, with little yellow teddy bears dancing around the edges. The napkins each had a yellow bear holding a pink and blue umbrella. Over the umbrella were written the words "It's a baby shower!"

We all agreed they were perfect, and Sabrina offered to keep them at her house until Saturday so my mother wouldn't see them.

By the time I got home, I had decided that Katie was right. I definitely had to talk to my parents. After all, how could I expect them to understand how I was feeling if I didn't try to explain?

I decided to wait until after Charlie was in bed, when things would be quieter.

I found my parents sitting and talking with Nooma and my grandfather in the living room. They all looked so warm and comfortable sitting there. There was a fire going in the fireplace. My grandparents were sitting on the love seat, and I saw that my grandfather had his hand on my grandmother's knee. My parents were sitting in two separate chairs, but my father was leaning very close to my mother.

". . . So there was quite a lot to take care of," my father was saying when I walked into the room. "It was a big job putting all her papers in order."

"I remember Margie Birdsong from when we lived on the reservation," said Nooma.

I sat down on one of the chairs next to my mother. "Who are they talking about?" I asked my mother quietly.

"An old woman died out on the reservation," my mother told me. "Your father went out there to settle her things."

I sat back to listen to the conversation. Somehow it didn't seem like the best moment to bring up what I wanted to talk about.

"Margie had a granddaughter living with her, didn't she?" asked Nooma. "How old is the little girl now?"

My father smiled. "Well, actually, the granddaughter's a pretty big girl now. Eighteen."

"How time flies!" exclaimed my grandmother, shaking her head.

"Smart girl, too," said my father. "She just got a scholarship to attend Acorn Falls Community College."

I shifted in my seat. It was beginning to seem like it wasn't going to be easy to change the subject.

"Well, if she's going to college, then she can't stay on at the reservation," said my mother. "It's forty miles one way. That's much too far to travel to classes every day."

"Yes, I know," answered my father. "I told her I'd try to help her find a room somewhere here in town."

I cleared my throat, hoping that I might be able to get their attention, but no one seemed to notice.

"She was always a very sweet little girl, as I remember," said Nooma. "What's her name again?"

"Mary," said my father. "Mary Birdsong."

Even though I had hoped to be talking about something else, I couldn't help noticing what a pretty name that was. That's one of the great things about Chippewa names. Very often they're related to things in nature. My own last name, Cloud, is like that, too.

"Eighteen's awfully young to be completely on her own," my mother said.

"Yes," agreed my father. "But she seems like a very responsible girl. She'll probably need some kind of a job, too, to pay for schoolbooks and other expenses."

I stood up. It seemed like they were all going to go on talking about this Mary Birdsong for quite a while, so I decided to go upstairs and do some homework. I'd just have to find some other time to talk to them.

The delivery of baby furniture my mother and Nooma had picked out last week at the Widmere Mall had just arrived that day, and a lot of it was already in my room, so things were kind of crowded in there.

I made my way around the crib and slid between the changing table and the new chest of drawers to my roll-top desk. There was barely enough space to pull my chair out and sit down. I hoped the builders would have my new room finished soon so I could move in.

I decided to work on my essay about the Elizabeth Barrett Browning poem for school. Before I knew it, I was completely involved in my work, and I had forgotten all about not being able to talk to my parents.

The more I went over the beautiful lines of poetry, the more I forgot about my problems. Eventually I even forgot about the baby furniture that was piled up all around me.

Chapter Nine

"Can somebody hand me that roll of pink crepe paper?" Sabrina called out, straining to reach the top of the arched doorway between my family's dining room and living room. She was wearing a cropped purple T-shirt and a denim miniskirt with purple anklet socks and red suede flats. Tied in her curly auburn hair as a headband was a wide piece of white lace.

Katie, who was wearing a pink-and-white-striped cotton T-shirt dress with a matching pink ribbon around her ponytail, hurried over to Sabrina with the roll of crepe paper.

"Are you sure you don't want me to do that for you, Sabs?" I asked, looking up at her. "It would probably be a lot easier for me to reach."

"No, that's okay," she answered. "You go ahead with what you're doing."

I went back to unwrapping the packages of teddy bear plates and napkins and stacking them on our dining room table. It was finally Saturday, the day of the baby shower. I was dressed in a bright yellow cotton sweater and a black-and-white-plaid miniskirt with black tights and black flats. My hair was held back by a wide, stretchy, bright yellow headband.

My father had taken my mother to the movies, and we were all rushing to get things ready before they got back. There had been one really scary moment when my mother had started to tell my father that she didn't think they should go because she had too much to get done around the house, but my father had talked her into it.

Suddenly I heard a loud bang.

"Aaaah!" screamed Sabrina. "What was that?"

"Ooops," said Randy, who was sitting on the living room floor, surrounded by pink and blue balloons. "I guess I blew that one up a little too much."

Just then Nooma came out of the kitchen with Charlie close behind her. In her hands was a big platter.

"The cookies are done," she said, setting the platter down on the table.

"I helped decorate them!" said Charlie proudly.

I looked at the cookies, which were each decorated with pale pink or blue icing and multicolored sprinkles.

"They look great," I said.

"Yeah," said Charlie, reaching for a cookie.

"Not yet, young man," said Nooma, taking his outstretched hand in hers, "or there won't be any left for the party. Besides, I still need your help with the rest of the food in the kitchen. Who else is going to lick the spoons for me?"

"I'll help you, Nooma," Charlie sang out happily, galloping back into the kitchen behind her.

Just then I heard the doorbell ring.

"That's Sam and the boys," Sabrina called out. "They said they'd come over early to help out."

"I'll get it," said Katie.

She opened the front door, and Sam, Nick, Jason, Billy, Michel, and Arizonna burst into the living room.

"Hey, where do we put our presents?" asked Sam.

"What should we do to help?" asked Billy.

"Wow," said Arizonna, walking over to the dining room table, "totally psychedelic cookies."

I made sure that everyone had something to do, and before we knew it, the place was ready. It looked great. Sabs and Katie had hung pink and blue crepe paper all over the room, and Randy's pink and blue balloons were tied in bunches everywhere. The banner that Katie, Sabs, Randy, and I had painted at Katie's house was strung across the middle of the living room. The presents were stacked in front of the fireplace, and the dining table was covered with Nooma's snacks. My grandfather had even brought in some flowers from the garden for a centerpiece.

"Oh, I almost forgot," said Randy, pulling a cassette tape out of the pocket of her black denim miniskirt. "My special baby shower music mix."

"Awesome, Randy," said Arizonna. "You make the best tapes."

"Well, I made this one especially for this party," said Randy, walking over to the stereo and inserting the tape into the tape deck. "I think you'll see what I mean."

The tape began to play, and I heard the first notes of "Baby Love," an old song by Diana Ross and the Supremes from the 1960s. I knew the song because they had played it at the seventh-grade sixties dance at Bradley a while ago.

"Great song, Randy!" said Sabs. "I love the Supremes."

"That's not all," said Randy. "Just wait."

The next song was called "Baby Face," and it was definitely older than the first song, but it sounded kind of familiar.

"I get it!" I said suddenly. "The songs all have the word *baby* in them."

"That's brilliant, Randy," said Katie.

"I used the computer over at the radio station," said Randy. I knew she was talking about KTOP 1350, the AM radio station over at Bradley High where she sometimes helps out. "I just programmed it to look up every song in the station's collection with the word *baby* in it."

Suddenly I noticed my grandfather stand up from his rocker and begin to dance around a little, clapping his hands and singing along. This must really be an old song, I thought, amazed that he knew all the words.

The next thing I knew, my grandfather had danced over to where my grandmother was sitting and was trying to pull her out of her chair to join him. Nooma scowled and tried to shoo him away at first, but then she gave in and stood up. Seeing the two of them dancing in each other's arms gave me a really warm feeling inside. And when I looked around at my friends, they were all watching my grandparents and smiling, too.

Then the doorbell began to ring, and the other guests began to arrive. Soon the living room was full of people, and the pile of presents in front of the fireplace was really big.

The next thing I knew, someone had spotted my father's car pulling into the driveway. Quickly we all arranged ourselves under the banner and waited for the front door to open.

My parents walked in, and as soon as my mother saw the banner, her eyes lit up. Then she looked at all of us with a really amazed expression on her face.

"How wonderful!" she said, walking through the archway from the front hall to the living room.

"Surprise, Mom," I said, walking toward her to give her a hug.

"Oh, Allison," she said, putting her arms around me and giving me a squeeze, "how thoughtful."

Suddenly I felt Charlie pulling on my sweater. I looked down at him.

"Come on, Allison," he said excitedly,

"Nooma says we can have cookies now!"

After everyone had eaten something and my mother had said hello to all the guests, we gathered around to watch her open the presents.

"My goodness," she said, sitting down in a chair near the fireplace and looking at the pile of presents, "I hardly know where to begin!"

"Here, Mom," I said, sitting on the edge of the footrest near her chair. "I'll hand them to you one at a time."

"Open mine, open mine!" said Sam, pushing a large green-and-white-striped box toward me.

I handed the box to my mother and watched her take off the paper. As she lifted the lid and peered inside, she got a funny look on her face.

"Well, thank you, Sam," she said, reaching into the box and pulling out a basketball.

"Sam!" cried Sabrina, staring wide-eyed at her twin. "You got a basketball for a baby?!"

"Hey, come on, Sabs," Sam answered, his face turning red, "he's not always going to be a baby. So when he gets old enough, I can teach him how to play."

"Or her," I pointed out.

"Oh, yeah, I guess that's right," said Sam.

"Well, I think it's a lovely present," said my

mother. "Straight from the heart, and that's what really counts. Thank you, Sam."

Sam smiled sheepishly.

"By the way, Mrs. Cloud," said Katie, "Sabrina, Randy, and I have a present for the baby, too."

"But it's not going to be ready for a little while," Sabs explained.

"Yeah," said Randy. "It's kind of hard to explain, but we can't give it to you yet."

My friends hadn't told me about their present, and I wondered what it could be.

"Well, I'm sure it will be very nice, whatever it is," said my mother, smiling. "It's obviously something you three have put a lot of thought into."

The next present was in a flat blue box with a white bow. It turned out to be a musical mobile to hang above the crib, from my Aunt Vivian. Next came Aunt Pauline's present, which was a set of rattles and rubber teething toys.

Then I reached for an unusual-looking present. The box was wrapped in newspaper which had been painted with purple and orange peace signs.

"That's from me," said Arizonna. "The wrapping paper is totally recycled to help save the planet."

"What a creative idea," said my mother, taking the present from me.

Inside the box was a tiny tie-dyed T-shirt and a matching pair of tie-dyed cotton booties.

"Aren't these something!" exclaimed my mother, holding them up for everyone to see.

"The way I see it, any new little member of the Cloud family is definitely going to be totally cool," Arizonna explained.

The next present was from Billy. It was flat and thin and I could tell right away that it must be a book. I looked over at him and smiled as I handed the package to my mother.

"Oh, this is wonderful," said my mother, taking the book out of the wrapping paper.

"It was my favorite when I was really little," Billy explained shyly.

"Well, I'm sure the baby will grow to love it, too," said my mother. "Thank you."

After my mother had finished opening the rest of the presents, and Nooma and I had cleaned up all the wrapping paper and ribbons, I picked up the book from Billy to see what it was.

"*Pat the Bunny,*" I read.

Suddenly I heard Billy's voice over my shoulder.

"My mother used to read it to me when I was little," he said. "It was my favorite. I used to ask for it every night."

I didn't know what to say. Billy's mother died five years ago, and I knew that he must really miss her. Suddenly I felt really lucky to have the family I do.

"There are lots of fun things for a baby to look at and touch inside," Billy went on with a smile.

"This is a really special present, Billy," I said, smiling back at him. "The baby is really lucky to have it."

"The baby's really going to be lucky to have you around to read it out loud," he said.

I was beginning to feel really excited. Soon there was going to be a new member of my family. A new person, who would be learning to talk, and read, and write. I wondered if my new brother or sister would turn out to love books the way I do. Who knows, maybe he or she would even end up being a poet someday.

The doorbell suddenly rang. I wondered who could be arriving at the party so late. Besides, everybody who was supposed to be there already was.

"Excuse me," I said to Billy, heading for the front door.

I opened the door and saw a big, burly man in coveralls. Behind him, parked in front of the house, was a truck with the words PICKWICK LANE FURNISHINGS written in script on the side.

"I've got your delivery here," said the man. "Where do you want it?"

"You must have the wrong house," I said. "We're not expecting anything."

He checked the slip of paper in his hand. "Cloud?" he asked.

"Yes," I said, "but —"

Just then I heard my father's voice behind me.

"I'll take care of that, Allison," he said.

"But, Dad —"

"In fact, I think Nooma needs your help in the kitchen right now," he told me.

I shrugged my shoulders and headed for the kitchen. The delivery was probably just something else for the baby's room, I decided. Although I couldn't think of another thing the baby needed.

But when I got to the kitchen, Nooma wasn't

even in there. That's strange, I thought, walking back into the living room. But the next thing I knew, I was cornered by Aunt Pauline and Aunt Vivian, who wanted to talk about how much I'd grown, and kept asking me questions about school.

Within a few minutes I had completely forgotten about the strange delivery.

Chapter Ten

Finally everyone was gone, my father and I had finished helping Nooma clean up, and my family was sitting in the living room. My mother was looking over the baby gifts, and my grandmother was crocheting a pair of booties. My grandfather relaxed in his rocker by the fireplace, and my father was looking through the newspaper. Even Charlie was pretty tired out and was quietly playing with a jigsaw puzzle on the rug. I decided it was probably a good time to talk to my family about how I had been feeling like I needed more time for myself.

It was funny, but I felt kind of nervous about bringing up the subject. I had never really asked my family for anything like this before, and I wasn't sure what they would say. What if they thought I was being selfish?

But then I heard Katie's words echoing in my head — "It's no good to just keep your feelings inside. If something is bothering you, you should talk to your parents about it." I knew she was right. How was my family ever going to know how I felt if I didn't tell them myself?

I walked into the living room and sat down on the couch next to my mother.

"Hello, sweetie," said my mother, smiling at me. "You must be exhausted from all the work you did for that wonderful party."

"I'd say it was a real hit," said my father, folding his newspaper. "You didn't suspect anything, did you, Meredith?"

"Not a thing," my mother answered. "I was totally surprised. You really planned a wonderful party, Allison."

"I didn't do it alone," I said. "Nooma really took care of the cooking, and Katie, Sabrina, and Randy all helped me a lot with everything else. Besides, it was fun."

"I didn't mind cooking," said Nooma, looking up from her crocheting. "It was all that dancing around with your grandfather that tired me out!"

I looked over at my grandfather, who had fallen asleep in his rocker.

"It looks like Grandpa tired himself out, too," I said.

"Well, it was a beautiful baby shower," said my mother. "I'm just amazed that you managed to pull this party together, Allison."

"Well, actually," I said, taking a deep breath, "speaking of the baby, there's something I wanted to talk to all of you about."

"What is it, honey?" asked my mother, looking at me with concern. "Is something upsetting you?"

"Well, sort of," I began. "I mean, I'm not really sure how to say this, but I've kind of been thinking about how things are going to be after the baby is born."

"Of course you have," said Nooma. "We're all thinking about that. There's a lot to do to get ready for a new baby."

"Is there something in particular that you've been thinking about?" my mother asked. "Something you want to tell us about?"

I took a superdeep breath. "Yes, there is," I said firmly. "I've been doing a lot of thinking about what it's going to be like to have another little brother or sister in the house. Of course, I'm really excited, just like everyone else. I know I'll love the baby a lot, just like I love Charlie. But there's something that's worrying me, too, and that is that I'll probably be spending a lot of time taking care of this baby, the way I take care of Charlie now."

"But you do a very good job taking care of Charlie," said Nooma.

"That's what worries me," I answered. "For a long time, I've been doing a good job taking care of Charlie whenever anyone needs me to. And I'm sure I'll do a good job taking care of the baby, too. But with two of them for me to take care of, I'm afraid I'm going to end up with a full-time baby-sitting job." I stopped and stared down at the floor. I was kind of embarrassed, but I knew I had to get everything off my chest.

"What I'm trying to say is, I think I need to be able to have a little more time to myself. To see my friends, or just to do some of the things that I need to do, for me."

There, I had said it. And suddenly I knew that Katie was right. No matter how my family reacted to what I had just said, I already felt much better having told them how I felt.

"I think I know how you feel," said my mother. "I know that we've all relied on you a lot, maybe too much."

After that no one said anything for a few

minutes. I still sort of felt embarrassed, but relieved.

"And I think I may have the solution to this entire problem," said my father.

We all just stared at him.

"Remember when I told you about Mary Birdsong, Margie Birdsong's granddaughter, out on the reservation?" he asked.

"Yes, of course," said my mother. "The girl with the full scholarship from Acorn Falls Community College."

"Well, as I mentioned, she wants to use that scholarship, but she needs a place to live here in town. She also needs a job." He looked at me. "So what I'm thinking is this — maybe Mary Birdsong would like to take over that full-time baby-sitting job from Allison."

"Oh, Nathan, what a wonderful idea," said my mother. "But where will she stay?"

"I've been doing some thinking about that, too," said my father. "I thought we might move my study downstairs to the storage room. You and Nooma have really done quite a job clearing the baby stuff out of there these last few weeks. What's left over can go down to the basement. I can move my desk down there, and then Mary can take my old study upstairs."

"That way she'll be close to the baby's room," agreed Nooma.

I couldn't believe what I was hearing. All I had asked for was a little more time to myself, and now it seemed like I might never have to baby-sit again if I didn't want to.

"That settles it," said my father. "I'll get in touch with Mary in the morning and see how soon she can be ready to move in. Meanwhile, I think it's about time Allison took a look at that delivery that came for her today."

"What delivery?" I asked, startled. Then I remembered the man who had come to the door during the party, and the truck parked outside. "For me?" I asked again. I wasn't expecting anything.

"Why don't you go take a look at it, honey," said my mother, smiling.

"Where is it?" I asked, standing up and looking around. What could they be talking about?

"It's up in your new room, of course!" said my father.

"My new room?" I repeated. "But it's not finished yet, is it?"

My mother just looked at me and smiled, and

I saw my father wink at her. As fast as I could, I ran up the stairs and down the hall to the door to my new room. I had checked the room every day, but it was usually covered with dropcloths and full of workmen so that nothing looked finished to me.

I threw open the door and stepped inside. There it was — my room, completely finished! Of course, there was no furniture in it yet, and it hadn't been painted, but there were four complete walls, and three of them were filled with windows. I had been so busy with school and the shower I just hadn't been paying attention to the builders. Anyway, it was beautiful.

I headed toward the french door on the other side of the room, anxious to see the terrace. My mother was right. The door was a perfect touch. I stepped outside and looked around. The terrace was definitely cool. Suddenly I noticed a white wicker swing seat hanging in the far corner of the terrace. It looked just the right size to curl up in with a book, and the cushion was covered in a deep purple flowered fabric.

I sat down in the swing and looked over the wooden rail of the terrace at the garden below. Even though it was outside, the terrace was already my favorite part of my new room.

I ran back downstairs to my parents. I hugged my mother, then my father, then my grandmother.

"I love it! I love everything about my new room. It's perfect!" I cried. "Thank you so much!"

"Me too! Me too!" yelled Charlie, jumping up from his spot on the floor.

"Yes, Charlie, I especially love *you*!" I scooped him into my arms and gave him a big hug.

"The moment I saw that swing I knew you had to have it for your new room," my mother said. "I know how much you love your window seat, and yet you never said a thing about having to give it up." I looked at my mother and smiled. She seemed to understand me best of all.

"The terrace is just the right spot for it," said my grandmother. "But we may have to get a matching one for the backyard."

"I think you're right, Nooma," I said and hurried over to Nooma to give her a kiss on the cheek. "The terrace is perfect, the whole room is perfect!" I cried to no one in particular.

Just then my grandfather, who was still in his chair by the fireplace, opened his eyes.

"Eh, eh," he said, clearing his throat. "What's

going on? I thought the party was over."

"It is over for us," said my grandmother, walking over to my grandfather. "It's time for you and me to go back to our place and call it a night. Have a good evening, all." And my grandparents walked out of the room.

"You too, Charlie," said my father.

"Aaaaawwww." Charlie scowled. "It's still early."

"I think it's time we all went to bed," said my mother. "It's been a long day for everyone."

I was so excited that I decided to sleep in my new room that night, even though it was still empty. My father helped me drag my mattress down the hall from my old room and put it on the floor.

Lying in bed in the dark, I could see the stars through the windows all around me. Every once in a while a gentle breeze brushed the branches of the big chestnut tree against my roof, and the sound lulled me into a deep, deep sleep.

Sometime in the middle of the night I was disturbed by the sound of pounding. I started to have a dream that it was the builders, working on my room. But suddenly I remembered that my room was already finished, and that I was lying in it. I woke up and realized that someone was pounding on the door.

"Allison! Wake up!" my father exclaimed.

I jumped out of bed and ran to open the door. My father was standing in the hall, wearing a pair of pants with his pajama top.

"What is it? What's wrong?" I asked breathlessly.

"It's time," he told me. "I'm taking your mother to the hospital. She's going to have the baby!"

Chapter Eleven

The next morning Allison calls Randy.

ALLISON: Hi, Katie, it's Allison.

KATIE: Hi, Allison. Where have you been all morning? I've been trying to call you. I wanted to tell you how much I enjoyed the baby shower.

ALLISON: Well, I just got back from the hospital!

KATIE: You're kidding! Your mom had the baby?!

ALLISON: That's right! I now have a little baby sister.

KATIE: Oh, Allison, that's great. What's her name?

ALLISON: Well, my parents weren't really sure what name they wanted. So I had an idea, and it turns out they loved it.

KATIE: What?

ALLISON: Barrett Cloud.

KATIE: Oh, Allison, that's so pretty.

ALLISON: I think so, too. I named her after Elizabeth Barrett Browning. By the way, Katie?

KATIE: Yes?

ALLISON: Well, I just wanted to tell you that you were right about talking to my parents. I explained how I felt, and they completely understood. In fact, they're getting someone to come live with us to help take care of Charlie and Barrett so I won't have to spend so much time baby-sitting.

KATIE: Allison, that's wonderful. Who is it?

ALLISON: Her name is Mary Birdsong, and she's eighteen years old. Right now she lives on the Chippewa Reservation where my father grew up, but she's going to go to college here in Acorn Falls and she needs a place to stay.

KATIE: That sounds perfect. I'm really happy for you, Allison.

ALLISON: Thanks, Katie. And thanks for everything. Listen, I'd better go. My father's taking us all out to dinner to celebrate.

KATIE: Okay. Do you want me to call Sabs and Randy to let them know the news?

ALLISON: Could you? That would be great. I'm kind of tired and wanted to get a nap first.

KATIE: Sure, no problem.

ALLISON: Oh, Katie, could you especially tell Randy, I'll call her later tonight.

KATIE: Sure. Bye, Al.

ALLISON: Bye!

Katie calls Sabrina.

(There is the sound of a scuffle and the telephone dropping on the floor.)

SABRINA: Sam! I said I'd get it!

SAM: Well, I got here first!

SABRINA *and* SAM *together:*
Hello?

KATIE: Hello? Sabrina? Is that you?

SABRINA: *(Wrestling the phone away from Sam)* See, Sam, I told you it was for me! Hello, Katie?

KATIE: Sabrina, I have great news! Allison's mother had a baby girl!

SABRINA: That's fantastic. Allison must be so happy. Did you find out what her name is?

KATIE: Yes, it's Barrett. Barrett Cloud. Al named her after Elizabeth Barret Browning.

SABRINA: Oooh, how romantic! Well, I guess we can get the present now. I'll call Randy and let her know. Maybe the three of us can go back to that store we found on Carlyle Street after school tomorrow.

KATIE: That sounds good. See you tomorrow, Sabs.

SABRINA: Bye, Katie.

Sabrina calls Randy.

RANDY: Hello?

SABRINA: Randy, what took you so long? I was about to hang up.

RANDY: Oh, I was practicing my drums and I couldn't hear the phone. It's a good thing I decided to take a

	break.
SABRINA:	It sure is! Randy, I've got the most incredible news.
RANDY:	What's up?
SABRINA:	Allison's mother had the baby! It's a girl!
RANDY:	Awesome! Did you find out what the name is?
SABRINA:	Yes, it's Barrett.
RANDY:	Cool name.
SABRINA:	Barrett Cloud. Isn't that beautiful? Anyway, I talked to Katie, and the three of us are going to go to that store on Carlyle Street tomorrow after school to get the baby present.
RANDY:	Sounds good, Sabs.
SABRINA:	Okay, Randy, see you in school tomorrow.
RANDY:	Bye.

Chapter Twelve

"My goodness, what a heavy little thing you are!" said my mother, shifting the baby from one arm to the other.

"Here, Mom, I'll hold her for a while," I volunteered, walking out into the garden where my mother was sitting with Barrett.

"All right, here you go, sweetheart," said my mother, gently handing over the baby, who was wrapped in a white cotton blanket.

I looked down at the bundle in my arms. My mother and Barrett had been home from the hospital for two weeks, but I still couldn't quite believe that now I had a sister.

"Hi there, Barrett," I said quietly, looking down into her pink little face. I reached out to touch her hand and felt her tiny fingers close around one of mine. Her fingernails were so small, they almost didn't seem real.

As I gently rocked her in my arms, Barrett let

out a little yawn, and soon her eyes began to close.

Just then my father stuck his head out of the french doors from the living room.

"I'm leaving for the reservation now to pick up Mary Birdsong and her things," he said. "Anyone want to come along?"

"I'll go with you, Dad," I said, walking over to my mother to give her the baby. "I think Barrett's starting to fall asleep, anyway."

"Yes, it's about that time," said my mother.

"I'll take her upstairs and put her down for a nap. Meredith, I think you could use this time to get a nap yourself," said Nooma.

"Sounds good to me, Nooma," said my mother, yawning. "An hour or so's nap won't hurt."

My grandmother took the baby from Mom, and they headed upstairs.

"I just have to make sure I'm back by three o'clock," I told my father. "That's when Randy, Katie, and Sabrina said they were coming over. They said they have a present for the baby."

My father glanced down at his watch. "Great. I don't think that'll be a problem," he said. "We have plenty of time to get out to the reservation and back."

"I'm just going to run upstairs to get a sweater," I said. "I'll meet you in the car."

I hurried up the stairs and down the hall to my new room. Inside, I just had to stop and admire it again. Now that the walls and ceiling had been painted, and the furniture had been moved in, it really did look beautiful. My mother had even let me go and pick out my new curtains and bedspread by myself. Well, my father drove Nooma and me to the store. But they loved what I had chosen.

I had pushed my roll-top desk up against one set of windows so I could have a view of the chestnut tree while I did my homework. On one side of the door, against the one wall without windows, were my bookshelves and my big wooden chest of drawers. The headboard of my bed was pushed up against the other side of that wall, so when I lay in bed at night I could see the stars coming through the windows on all three sides.

I grabbed a green cardigan sweater from the chest of drawers and headed out the other door onto the terrace. Taking just a minute to admire the white wicker swing hanging in the corner, I skipped down the stairs to the backyard, and around the side of the house to where my father was waiting in the car.

I hadn't been out to the reservation since last summer, when my parents took the whole family to the Chippewa Cultural Festival. The festival is like a big fair that the reservation has every year. It's a lot of fun; there are performances of traditional Chippewa songs and dances, and arts and crafts displays, and a lot of really good food. My father always says it's important for Charlie and me to experience that kind of stuff, and I agree. I guess soon it will be time for Barrett to start learning about Chippewa customs and traditions, too.

As we drove out of Acorn Falls, there were fewer and fewer houses. In a little while we were surrounded by farmland, with only an occasional house or barn in sight.

In a little less than an hour, we turned off the main road and onto a bumpy dirt road. Soon we passed a wooden sign announcing that we were entering the reservation.

I always feel kind of funny when I'm visiting the reservation. In one way, it feels good to be in a place where there are so many Native American Indians. But in another way, the reservation is kind of a sad place. Especially when you think about the fact that most Chippewa people don't get to leave the reservation and live anywhere else.

I wondered if Mary Birdsong had spent much time away from the reservation, and how she would like living in Acorn Falls.

Just then my father slowed the car in front of a group of unpainted wooden buildings.

"We're supposed to meet Mary at the general store," my father explained, pulling up into the dirt parking lot.

Just then I noticed a girl sitting on the front step of one of the buildings. She looked a few years older than me, and she was wearing blue jeans and a plain white T-shirt. Her straight black hair was tied back in a braided bun at the base of her neck, and around her neck were several strands of tiny multicolored beads. Next to her on the ground were two worn-looking green suitcases.

How could anyone fit everything they owned into two suitcases, I wondered.

"There she is," said my father, stepping out of the car. "Hello, Mary!" he called, heading toward the girl, who stood up and waved back.

I got out and walked over to where my father

and the girl were standing.

"Mary, I'd like you to meet my daughter Allison," said my father. "Allison, this is Mary Birdsong."

Mary smiled. "Hi, Allison," she said.

"Hi, Mary," I said, smiling back.

"Well, let's take care of these suitcases," said my father, reaching for the one nearest to him. As he picked it up, he groaned. "Oooof! What do you have in here, Mary — rocks?"

"Actually, Mr. Cloud, that one's full of books," Mary said sheepishly.

I turned to look at her. This Mary Birdsong seemed like she might just turn out to be a very interesting person.

On the way home in the car, I told Mary a little bit about our family.

"Charlie can be a little wild," I warned her, "but he's a sweetie once you figure out how to handle him."

When we got home, it seemed like Charlie was already working on living up to his reputation. As we walked in the door, he came charging down the stairs with a patch over one eye and a plastic sword in his hand.

"I'm a pirate! I'm a pirate! Watch out!" he

yelled. And came right up to Mary.

My mother and grandmother came hurrying down the stairs after him.

"Charlie! Charlie!" Nooma hissed. "I thought I told you to keep it down. You'll wake Barrett."

"But I'm a pirate!" he yelled again. "Pirates never have to be quiet!"

"Charlie," said my father in a stern voice. "It's time to quiet down now and let your baby sister sleep. Besides, there's someone here I want you to meet. Charlie, Meredith, Nooma, this is Mary."

"Hello, everyone. Hi, Pirate Charlie," said Mary with a smile. Then she turned and bent closer to Charlie. "Hey, I'll bet if you're a real pirate, then you probably have a secret hideout somewhere."

"What do you mean, secret hideout?" asked Charlie, lowering his sword.

"Oh, you know," said Mary, "someplace really special that's just for you."

"Well," said Charlie, interested, "I do have my tree house . . ."

"That's perfect," said Mary. "Why don't you take me and show me your tree house. I'd love to see it."

"Okay," said Charlie, leading her out the front

door. "It's over this way."

My parents, Nooma, and I stood in the front hall and stared at each other in astonishment.

"That looks like the beginning of a match made in heaven," joked my father.

"I'm impressed," said my mother.

I didn't know what to say. For the first time in what seemed like forever, I didn't have to take care of anyone but myself.

Then, suddenly, I thought of exactly what I wanted to say.

"I think I'll go up to my room for a while," I announced happily.

A little while later, I heard someone coming up the stairs, and then I heard a knock on my door.

"Hey!" said Sabrina, stepping into the room. "Cool room, Al!"

"Hi, Sabs," I said happily, replacing my bookmark and closing my book.

In a moment Katie appeared, holding a brown teddy bear with a pink-and-white bow. Close behind her was Randy, who had a large box in her hand. It was wrapped in yellow paper that had toys all over it.

"Wow, Allison!" exclaimed Sabrina, opening

the french doors that led onto the terrace. We all followed her outside.

"This is amazing!" Randy exclaimed.

"I love it," agreed Katie. "Especially the swing."

"Come on in and see the rest," I said, opening the door and leading them back into my room.

"This is great," said Randy, walking over to the window by the chestnut tree. "It kind of reminds me of the wrap-around view from my father's old office in New York. Except that that was thirty-nine stories up. And there weren't any trees."

"The colors we all chose look great in here," said Katie.

Sabrina looked at me with a serious expression on her face.

"Allison," she said, "this is absolutely, positively the best room I have ever seen. It's better than anything in any of my magazines. In fact, this is the kind of room that should be in a magazine. I bet you could get it in one if you tried."

I couldn't help beaming. Now my room was truly perfect because my friends loved it, too.

"I don't know about all that, Sabs," I answered. "But I know I love it. And I'm happy you guys do, too."

"So," said Randy. "Where's Barrett? Can we see her?"

"We brought her present," said Katie, indicating the box in Randy's hands.

"And a teddy bear," said Sabs.

"Well," I said, "she's sleeping, so we'll have to be very quiet. But I guess we can take a look."

We walked carefully down the hall, opened the door to my old room, and peeked inside. My parents had done it over, too. It had pretty pink-and-white wallpaper and frilly pink curtains at the bay window.

"Wow, Al," said Sabs. "It's so weird that this isn't your room anymore."

"Do you miss it at all?" asked Katie.

"Are you kidding?" asked Randy. "With that great new room she has?"

I thought a moment.

"At first I thought I was going to miss the old room a lot," I said. "This room meant a lot to me, and I was pretty attached to it, especially my window seat. Then it turned out that my new room was really special, too."

"That's for sure," agreed Sabs.

"But there's another thing," I said. "Now that

this is Barrett's room, I can look forward to watching her grow up in it. Thinking about that makes me miss it a lot less."

I pushed open the door a little more and tiptoed into the room, with Katie, Randy, and Sabs right behind me.

"There she is," I whispered, leaning over the white bassinet where Barrett was sleeping.

"Oooooohhhh," whispered Sabrina, "she's so cute."

"She looks so peaceful," said Katie.

"She's so little," marveled Randy.

"Here, Allison," said Katie, pushing the gift-wrapped box toward me, "why don't you open her present for her."

I took the box from her and slipped off the lid. Inside, wrapped in white tissue paper, was a pillow. I pulled it out and looked at it.

I had never seen anything like it. Stitched across the pillow in puffy pink letters was the name BARRETT, and surrounding the letters on all sides were puffy white clouds on a pale blue background.

"This is beautiful," I said, looking at my three friends. "Where did you get it?"

"We had it made," said Randy.

"At this neat little store on Carlyle Street," added Katie.

"That's why we didn't have it ready for the shower," explained Sabrina. "We had to wait to find out what Barrett's name was going to be."

Suddenly I realized something I hadn't thought of before. In a way, I had given Barrett a gift, too — something that she would keep forever. I mean, if you thought about it, my gift to Barrett was her name.

Carefully, I placed the pillow on the window seat that had once been mine. Who knows, I thought, maybe someday Barrett will sit here to write poetry, too.

Don't Miss
GIRL TALK #22
PROBLEM DAD

"So, do you want to hear my good news first, or my bad news?" I asked as I approached a table in the cafeteria the next day.

"Better start with the bad, Randy," Al advised, pulling out a chair.

Sabs dropped into a chair next to Al. "No, do the good," she argued. "It'll be more fun."

"I think I'll wait until Katie gets here," I said. "Then I can tell you all at once. I was trying to get your attention during homeroom, but you guys were so busy listening to the announcements, I couldn't get a word in edge-wise."

Honestly, I don't pay much attention to announcements. I figure if there's something important going on (which, take my word for it, is rare), Sabs or Al will always clue me in.

I opened my lunch bag and pulled out my blueberry yogurt and the pita-and-cheese sand-wich I'd slapped together that morning.

Katie arrived at the table carrying her lunch tray. "Another U.F.O. for hot lunch," she said with a groan. "Unidentifiable Food Object."

"So what's your news, Randy?" Al asked.

I broke into a smile. "D's coming here to visit!" D's my father.

"Randy, that's awesome!" Sabs exclaimed. "When's he getting here?"

"Next week." As I said it, I realized that I didn't quite believe it myself.

"But that's not all!" I continued. "You'll never guess *why* he's coming to Acorn Falls — besides wanting to see me, of course. I'll give you a hint. It's not for the Acorn Falls night-life."

"Is he moving here?" Sabs ventured.

"No way, Sabs," Katie said as she ripped open a bag of potato chips. "Somehow I can't see Mr. Zak producing music videos in Acorn Falls."

"Well, how about commercials? Uh, make that *one* commercial," I said, grinning.

"Ohmygosh! He's going to shoot a commercial here? In Acorn Falls?" Sabs cried, nearly choking on her carrot stick. "This is the most awesome, most amazing, most excellent news!"

"It's great news, Randy. You must be so happy," Al said.

I had to admit I was feeling very pleased. "*And* D made me promise to invite you all to the filming. He's doing another Cubex jeans commercial. Hey, he had one other major piece of news. He broke up with Leighton."

"You don't suppose —" Sabs began. She stopped herself and shook her head so hard her curls nearly went into orbit. "Never mind," she added, glancing at me, then concentrating on her sandwich.

I was pretty sure I knew what she'd been about to say. "You were thinking maybe M and D could get back together now, weren't you?" I asked.

"Well, it would be so romantic," Sabs said with a sigh. "I mean, your dad will be here visiting, and who knows? One thing might lead to another. Anything could happen."

"You know, Randy," Sabs continued, "this could mean two weddings in one year! First Katie's mom, and now maybe yours!"

"What's wrong, Randy?" Al asked.

"M went on a date last night," I muttered.

TALK BACK!
TELL US WHAT YOU THINK ABOUT GIRL TALK BOOKS

Name _____

Address _____

City _____ State _____ Zip_____

Birthday _____ Mo._____ Year _____

Telephone Number (____)_____

1) Did you like this GIRL TALK book?

Check one: YES_____ NO_____

2) Would you buy another GIRL TALK book?

Check one: YES_____ NO_____

If you like GIRL TALK books, please answer questions 3-5; otherwise, go directly to question 6.

3) What do you like most about GIRL TALK books?

Check one: Characters_____ Situations_____
Telephone Talk_____Other_____

4) Who is your favorite GIRL TALK character?

Check one: Sabrina_____ Katie_____ Randy_____
Allison_____ Stacy_____ Other (give name) _____

5) Who is your *least* favorite character?

_____

6) Where did you buy this GIRL TALK book?

Check one: Bookstore____Toy store____Discount store____
Grocery store____Supermarket____Other (give name)_____

Please turn over to continue survey.

7) How many GIRL TALK books have you read?

Check one: 0____   1 to 2____   3 to 4 ____   5 or more____

8) In what type of store would you look for GIRL TALK books?

Bookstore_____Toy store_____Discount store_____

Grocery store_____Supermarket_____Other (give name)_____

9) Which type of store would you visit most often if you wanted to buy a GIRL TALK book?

Check *only* one: Bookstore_____Toy store_____

Discount store_____Grocery store_____Supermarket_____

Other (give name)_____

10) How many books do you read in a month?

Check one: 0____   1 to 2____   3 to 4 ____   5 or more____

11) Do you read any of these books?

Check those you have read:

The Babysitters Club_____   Nancy Drew_____

Pen Pals_____ Sweet Valley High _____

Sweet Valley Twins_____Gymnasts_____

12) Where do you shop most often to buy these books?

Check one: Bookstore_____Toy store_____

Discount store_____Grocery store_____Supermarket_____

Other (give name)_____

13) What other kinds of books do you read most often?

_____

14) What would you like to read more about in GIRL TALK?

_____

_____

Send completed form to :

GIRL TALK Survey, Western Publishing Company, Inc.

1220 Mound Avenue, Mail Station #85

Racine, Wisconsin 53404

LOOK FOR THESE OTHER AWESOME GIRL TALK BOOKS!

MORE GIRL TALK TITLES TO LOOK FOR

Nonfiction

ASK ALLIE 101 answers to your questions about boys, friends, family, and school!

YOUR PERSONALITY QUIZ Fun, easy quizzes to help you discover the real you!

BOYTALK: HOW TO TALK TO YOUR FAVORITE GUY